Bathtime fo
And Other Stories

written and illustrated by
MARY RAYNER

COLLINS
PICTURE LIONS

Contents

First published in Great Britain by
William Collins Sons & Co. Ltd in 1986

First published in Picture Lions in 1989

Picture Lions is an imprint of the Children's Division,
part of the Collins Publishing Group,
London W1X 3LA

Lettuce is Too Flat first appeared in *Cricket* Magazine in November 1983

Printed by Warners of Bourne and London

Lettuce is Too Flat

One by one the piglets blinked and stirred. They began to get up and dress, but Benjamin Pig stayed asleep, a small hump under the checked blanket, only his snout showing.

"Wake up, Ben!" shouted the other piglets. "You'll make us all late!"

Benjamin opened his eyes, but he felt cross and at odds with himself and everyone else. Why should he get up? Everything he did had to fit in with the others. He and Garth had to wait in the cold outside *their* school in the afternoons, he had to watch the programmes on television that *they* liked, and he had to play the games that *they* chose.

Today he was going to do what *he* wanted. When Mrs Pig came upstairs to get him dressed, he wouldn't put on his blue shirt and insisted on a purple striped one. He shouted that his trousers were too loose and took clean ones out of the drawer, even though the others were hardly worn. And he refused point-blank to put on a jersey at all.

It was the same all day. When Garth was picked up to play with friends, they asked if Benjamin would like to come too, but he said no. He stayed at home and played his own games that morning, and at lunchtime the trouble started all over again.

Mother Pig opened the fridge door and took out some beetroot.

"Don't want beetroot," said Benjamin.

Mrs Pig tried again. "What about a nice carrot?"

"Don't want carrot."

She took a deep breath. "Perhaps some lettuce?"

"Lettuce is too flat," shouted Benjamin. "And I don't want any lunch at all." He threw his mug at the wall so that milk spilt everywhere.

"All right," said Mrs Pig, her patience at an end. "No lunch." She cleared up the milk and brewed herself a cup of tea. Benjamin flung himself down on the floor and began to cry. Mother Pig bent down to cuddle him, but he pushed her away. He lay in a corner by himself and played with his favourite car.

When it was three o'clock and time to start out to collect the other piglets from school, Benjamin had begged a couple of biscuits from his mother, but that was all he had eaten. He refused to sit in his push-chair and dawdled along after her so slowly that they were late.

Sarah Pig was already out of the school gate and came scurrying towards them. She took one look at Benjamin's tear-stained face and the empty push-chair and knew that there had been trouble.

"Come on, Ben," said Mrs Pig. "Let's find the other piglets."

"No, don't want to."

Sarah was in a hurry for her tea. Catching her mother's eye across Ben's head, she whispered, "Wait, Mum, let me try." She bent down towards Ben.

"Hullo, Ben," she said.

Ben said nothing. He scowled at her.

"I don't want to collect the other piglets, do you, Ben?"

"Yes I do," said Benjamin.

"Let's go without them."

"No, don't want to."

"And when we get home I don't want any tea at all," said Sarah. "I don't want Mum to make any at all."

"Yes I do," shouted Benjamin. "I want *loads* of tea."

"All right," said Sarah. "And now I think I'll sit in the push-chair and have a ride home."

"No, you can't have it," said Benjamin, climbing in quickly. "It's mine."

Before he could change his mind, Mother Pig
had pushed him up to the school gate, gathered
up the others, and hurried home. And no one
had ever seen Benjamin eat so much.

Piglets and Pancakes

One day Mrs Pig was trying to make the piglets'
beds. She balanced unsteadily with her hind legs
on the second bunk and struggled to reach the
far side of the top one to tuck in the blankets.

"Bother these bunks," she muttered. As she
spoke, she missed her footing and slipped.
Grabbing at the blanket, she landed heavily on
the floor, taking all the bedding with her.

"This is the last time I make these beds. Sorrel! Bryony! Where are you?"

Sorrel and Bryony's faces appeared on the landing below, looking enquiring.

"In future you will make your own beds," said Mother Pig. "And call Sarah and Hilary and Cindy."

The faces turned sulky. "Why should we have to, when the boys don't?" asked Bryony. "It's not fair."

"Fair or not, I am not making them any longer."

Sorrel went upstairs grumbling. Mrs Pig rounded up Hilary and Cindy and Sarah and sent them up too. In the top attic the five girl piglets made their beds and then Sorrel said, "The boys ought to be made to do theirs."

"But they help Dad with the digging and things like that," said Cindy. "I think it's fair for us to do one kind of job and the boys to do another. Girls are good at some things and boys at others."

"Ooh, Cindy!" said Sorrel in a shocked voice. "You'll be saying next that boys are cleverer and stronger than girls."

"No, I didn't say that at all, I just know I'd rather make beds than dig."

"Well, I wouldn't," said Sorrel. "Or at least I'd like to be allowed to choose. Girls are as strong as boys any day."

"Oh no, they're not," said William, coming into the bedroom at that moment. "Prove it."

Sorrel was silent. Then she said, "All right, we'll have a sports day. Boys against girls. You wait and see. And we'll finish up with a tug of war, just to show you."

"Done," said William.

The girl piglets spent all morning planning the sports and writing out programmes. There would be races round the garden, a sack race, an egg and spoon race, a jumping competition, a pancake race, and then the final tug of war. Mrs Pig and Sorrel mixed a great bowl of batter for the pancakes.

"What's a pancake race?" asked Garth.

"You each have a pan with a pancake, and you have to run along as fast as you can and toss the pancake up in the air so that it turns over and lands back in the pan on its other side," explained Sorrel.

Garth pulled a face. It did not sound very easy to him, but William was grinning a pigletish grin. He wasn't thinking about the pancake race, he was thinking about the tug of war.

At last everything was ready. "Father Pig will have to be the judge," they decided.

The first race was the running race. Father Pig stood at the side of the lawn with a handkerchief raised.

"Go!" he bellowed, and down came the handkerchief.

The piglets tore down the garden, turned sharply round the potato patch at the far end, and panted back to the winning post. William was first. He was by far the quickest, but when it came to being careful in the egg and spoon race, he was not so good.

This time it was Sarah who won, with Cindy and Toby in second place together.

The sack race ended in laughter. It began well enough, with all ten piglets leaping along in their sacks, but after about three leaps Garth fell over, and then Benjamin fell over him, and Sorrel jumped sideways into Bryony, and pretty soon Mother and Father Pig had to untangle a mountain of squealing sacks. Nobody won.

The jumping went on a long time, with the rope raised higher each round. Garth and Benjamin were out, of course, right at the beginning because of their short little legs, but the others battled it out. Finally the highest jump was made by Hilary.

"There you are!" chanted Sorrel, dancing up and down. "We're winning, I told you so!"

"Just you wait," said William. "We'll show you."

When it came to the pancake race, Mother Pig lined them all up across the lawn with their pans. "One, two, three, go!" she shouted.

Benjamin sat down and ate his. Garth hurled his pancake into the air. It landed kerflump across Toby's eyes. Blinded, Toby banged into William, and they both fell headlong, their pancakes tumbling out onto the grass. Cindy threw hers into the air and lunged to catch it. There was a crash as her pan hit Hilary's, and both pancakes landed on the ground.

Meanwhile, Bryony was doing well, catching hers neatly and keeping up a steady pace towards the winning post. Not far behind came Alun, having decided that one toss was enough, holding his pan straight out in front of him and running for dear life. Bryony turned to look over her shoulder and stumbled, so that Alun thundered past and reached the winning post inches in front of her.

"Hooray!" shouted all the boys.

"Ya, boo!" shouted all the girls.

"Shush," said Father Pig, adding up the score, while the smaller piglets crawled about on the grass, picking up bits of pancake and cramming them into their mouths.

"It's absolutely even," announced Mr Pig. "Everything depends on the tug of war. Come on, Mum, we've both got to join in now."

Mrs Pig rolled up her sleeves and took her place at one end of the rope with Sarah, Sorrel, Hilary, Bryony and Cindy. Father Pig made all the boys take the other side. He stood back.

"Take the strain," he said. They pulled the rope straight, and he tied his white handkerchief round it above the centre line on the grass.

"Heave!" he shouted, and ran round to the back of the boys' team.

Quickest off the mark, the girls yanked it a little to their side while Father Pig was running round to the back, but the boys soon recovered and pulled back again. The boys were using all their weight and strength. The girls dug their trotters into the soft grass and pulled for all they were worth. But it was no good, the boys were gaining. Slowly, inch by inch, the handkerchief was being pulled over to their side.

"Oh," gasped Mrs Pig.

"Uh," grunted Mr Pig.

"Heave," shouted Sorrel, and "Ee-ee," went the five girl piglets and Mrs Pig in one big pull. Back came the handkerchief across the mark, and now it was the boys who gave ground.

Then suddenly, Garth slipped on a piece of
pancake on the grass, and his feet shot from
under him. Over went the three piglets behind
him like a row of skittles, leaving only Mr Pig
and William upright. The rope yielded so
suddenly that the girls fell over too, landing in a

heap on top of Mrs Pig and bringing William and Father Pig crashing down too.

"We've won!" shouted all the girls.

"No, *we've* won!" shouted the boys.

"Quiet, I'm the judge," said Father Pig, getting to his feet and peeling bits of soggy batter off his trousers. "Nobody's won, it's a tie. But it's okay." He turned to Mrs Pig, who was sitting panting on the grass. "I'll make our bed from now on, and the boys will each make theirs too."

Mrs Pig put an arm round Sorrel and whispered in her ear, "That's victory. And who made the pancakes? You and I did!"

Bathtime
for Garth Pig

Mrs Pig had decided. No more evenings out,
leaving the piglets was too dangerous. Instead,
she would cheer herself up by asking everybody
in. They would have a party, a grown-ups' party
with wine and delicious food. And, she thought as
she washed up all by herself, she would make the
piglets help.

The ten piglets were all very excited when she

suggested it. Mr and Mrs Pig made a long list of
all the friends they would ask, and all the next week
Mrs Pig mixed and rolled and baked and chopped to make
ready the food. The piglets helped. They stirred
and licked and sloshed and spilt, but it all got done
in the end. The larder was filled with pies and flans,
and the fridge with jellies and mousses.

On the afternoon of the party the piglets were
sent upstairs. "But I want you all down here,
washed and in your best clothes, to hand round
the crisps when everybody comes. And please
remember your manners," said Mrs Pig.

Mr Pig tried out records to see if they would do.

"You're not going to *dance*?" asked Benjamin Pig, staring at him. William began to laugh.

"Go on upstairs," said Mr Pig huffily.

Mrs Pig counted out knives and plates into piles and put them on the table. Mr Pig went up to change.

The front door bell rang. "Oh bother, they're early," said Mrs Pig, snatching off her apron and running to the front door. "Do come in," she said, leading the visitors into the living room. Then she ran back to the kitchen.

William and Alun and Garth came downstairs
in their best clothes, not quite as clean as Mother
Pig had hoped. She gave them each two plates to
hold, one in each trotter, the only way of making
sure that the food actually reached the living room.

The door bell rang again, and Sorrel Pig hurried
to open it. There was a lady in a pink silk frock,
and another in a lot of make-up and a spangled dress
down to the floor. Sorrel could not remember where
she had seen the spangly lady before, but she seemed
to know her way about, and went straight to the
living room.

The rest of the piglets came down and more
and more guests arrived. Father Pig came
panting in. Very soon the room was filled with
smoke and chatter.

Garth Pig felt like a sardine. If the walls of the
room had been made of tin, he thought, they
would bend outwards, it was so full. A thin fog
floated over everyone's head. His eyes watered.
Bravely he held onto his plate of peanuts and tried
to squeeze through. Every now and then a grown-
up would bend down and speak to him.

"Hullo, Benjamin, thank you."

"I'm Garth."

"What? Oh yes, sorry, you've grown."

If I'd shrunk, thought Garth crossly, it might be worth pointing it out, but on and on it went, the talk and the laughter, louder and louder, and now music as well. William pushed his way through towards him. "We're to go to bed," he shouted, "Mum says."

Garth was wedged between a long black skirt and a billowing flowery one, behind a low table. He could not move. William disappeared through the door into the hall. Garth ate several peanuts now that no one was looking, and peered round. He couldn't see any of his other brothers and sisters.

He squeezed between the black skirt and the flowery one and held up his plate of peanuts to the tall lady in the spangled dress. She leaned down, her beads dangling onto the plate.

"No thank you, I don't eat peanuts. But my, you've grown into a fine plump piglet!" And she gave his cheek a playful pinch.

"Ow," said Garth. He looked round for Alun or Toby, but they seemed to have left the room.

"If you're looking for your brothers and sisters," said the lady helpfully, "I think they've gone up to bed."

She bent down towards him. She seemed to be wearing a very strong perfume. Even through the smoke it made Garth's nose tingle in an odd way, and he could feel the little bristles down his back stand on end. But he remembered his manners like a good little piglet, and said nothing.

The lady put a wet nose in his ear. "I'll take you up if you like, help give you your bath. I think your Mum and Dad are busy."

Garth put down his plate and reached up to take her paw. She pushed a way through the crowd towards the hall, and they went up the stairs together.

The lady led him into the bathroom, put the plug in and turned on the hot tap. "Not quite hot enough," she said, readjusting the water heater.

Steam filled the bathroom, but she didn't turn on the cold. Her sparkly dress was clinging to her, and her make-up was running down her nose. She began to hum a little song, and Garth gave a gasp. He had heard that tune before.

"Fried or boiled, baked or roast,
   Or minced with mushyrooms on toast?"
she sang.

In the meantime, upstairs in the bedroom with no grown-ups about, the other nine piglets had changed straight into their pyjamas and nighties without washing or cleaning their teeth.

Sorrel was climbing into the top bunk she shared with Bryony when she noticed Benjamin all by himself in the bottom one. "Where's Garth?" she asked.

"Still downstairs, I saw him," said William.

"Better go and get him," said Sorrel. "Come on, everyone," and they ran down the stairs.

On the first floor landing, in spite of the noise coming from below, they heard the tap running in the bathroom and saw steam coming out from under the door. They tried the handle but it was shut.

"Locked himself in again, I suppose," said William. "Push, everybody." They leaned against the door and it burst open.

"There you are!" said Sorrel to Garth, glancing up in surprise at the visitor beside him, who was just reaching across to the tap. Then she noticed the feet just showing beneath the spangled skirt, standing on the bathmat.

Sorrel moved quickly. She slipped forward, and bending down, snatched the bathmat out from under those feet. With a howl of dismay, the lady in the spangled dress fell with an enormous splash into the boiling hot bath.

But the spangled dress protected her. Scrabbling wildly, she shot out of the water, and before the other piglets had realised what was happening she had flung open the bathroom window and leaped to the ground below.

The piglets watched open-mouthed as the bedraggled figure hobbled away down the path, and the last they saw before the darkness swallowed her up was the glint of a sequin in the gloom. And she was not seen again for a very long time, but that is another story.